Gnome Alone

E.R.Reilly

Illustrated by
Janet Bates

PUBLISHED IN GREAT BRITAIN BY
SANTIAGO PRESS
PO BOX 8808
BIRMINGHAM
B30 2LR
E-mail for orders and enquiries: santiago@reilly19.freeserve.co.uk

Illustrations © Janet Bates 2005

ISBN 0-9539229-6-0

Printed and bound in India by
OM Authentic Media, P.O. Box 2190, Secunderabad 500 003
E-mail: printing@ombooks.org

An Introduction by the author

I am a very ordinary man. I live a very ordinary life. My hobby is playing rugby and it is a game of rugby that led me to discover that I had a very special talent. After playing a game of rugby on a bright sunny afternoon in early September I made my way home. That day was a perfectly normal Saturday (although I had stayed at the rugby club for quite a lot longer than I usually do). I arrived home several hours later than I was expected, only to find that I couldn't get into my house. I later found out that my wife was in the house but didn't answer the door to me because she was cross with me for being so late.

Because of this I decided to go and sit on the grass in my garden. It was there that the most fascinating thing happened. I discovered that I could talk to Garden Gnomes! As you can imagine, this was a life changing event for me. I learnt all about Gnome history and Gnome culture. The book that you are about to read is the result of long happy chats that I and my friend Alistair Blacklaws had because he too can talk to gnomes. This is the story of Lucky, the gnome who lived in Alistair's garden in

Tansoo House in Harborne in Birmingham. Lucky is a wonderful character. I have become very fond of him indeed and I think that when you have read his story you will grow fond of him too!

This is his story in his own words.

GNOME ALONE

All I could hear was a big thumping and banging noise. I could hear wood breaking and young men shouting. I was just an ordinary gnome living in an ordinary garden. This noise was the sound being made by some young men who were coming into the little garden where I lived. They jumped over the fence and they walked all over the flowers. Then one of them picked me up. He was laughing and shouting and he was making me very frightened indeed. He threw me to his friend and his friend was laughing as well. They may have thought that it was

funny, but I didn't. They ran off back to their car and took me with them. They blindfolded me and put me under the driver's seat. It was hard for me to understand what they were saying. They were saying strange words that I had not heard much before. I listened very carefully until I could understand them. One of them was called Colin. They were from a place called the Black Country. I was able to find out that they called themselves "Colin's yam-yam friends" and that the one who was the leader was called Colin Docherty.

I don't honestly think that they were bad humans. I think that they thought that

what they were doing was funny. They thought that it was just a bit of a laugh. You see, to them I was just a statue. They didn't know any better. To be honest, I think that they had been drinking spirituous liquors. I know that humans do that a lot and I don't know why they do it. Drinking spirituous liquors makes humans behave very badly indeed and they do things that they would not dream of doing without it.

I lay on that car floor feeling very scared indeed. I began to feel very sad as well as I began to realise what had happened.

I had been gnomenapped.

It was the most frightening experience of my life, I don't mind telling you. I had been living a beautiful life up until that time and now I didn't know what Colin and his yam-yam friends had planned for me. It was not knowing what was happening to me that was frightening. Yes, that was the most frightening thing about the whole experience.

I know that humans don't know very much about us and that's partly the reason why I am telling you my story. The main reason that I am telling you my story though is because almost any gnome will tell you that it is a really fascinating tale.

I'm going to tell you all about gnomes and I'm going to tell you all about me and what happened to me after I got gnomenapped. I am called Lucky now and I am going to tell you how I came to be known by that name.

There are just a few simple things that you need to know about gnomes in order to fully understand my story. You see, gnomes love fishing. There's nothing that we love better than to sit by a pond all day trying to catch as many gnomefish as we possibly can.

In the evening, we meet up in a local garden and we fry our fish. We love to sit around a little campfire and tell our stories. We love telling stories probably as much as we love fishing, if the truth be told.

I really must tell you about the one thing that we love more than anything else in the world and that is Naccorom. Naccorom is our special herb. Naccoram is one of those funny words that isn't spelt exactly as it sounds. It's actually pronounced nar-cor-om. We cook our fish in it, we drink it for tea and we use it as medicine. Gnomes are at their happiest when they have lots of

Naccorom and at their saddest when they have not got any at all.

Ours is a simple life and my life had been very simple indeed until that awful day that I was gnomenapped. For a very long time, I had lived in a little garden in a place called Harborne in Birmingham. Birmingham is a city in the middle of England and I must say that I had always been very happy there indeed. I lived in a house called Tansoo House. It was a very pleasant house with lots of music and laughter ringing out from its windows. It had a very nice human called Alistair who lived there with his friends.

And, best of all, you could always catch beautiful plump gnomefish.

I do have a distant memory of life before Birmingham though. I vaguely remember a time when I spent a good while living indoors. Gnomes hate being indoors - we can't get out by ourselves, you see. If

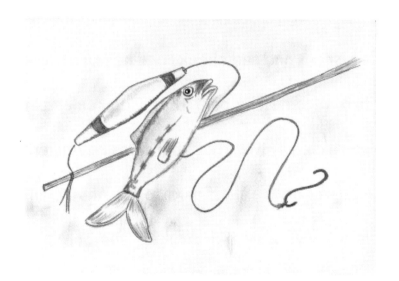

we are taken indoors by a human, a human needs to take us out again. I just about remember that I was in a shop. There was a lot of wood in the shop. Wooden counters, wooden shelves and wooden floorboards. I remember that a bell rang every time somebody opened the door and that there was a shopkeeper who had long grey whiskers and red cheeks and he wore a long brown coat. The part that I do remember quite clearly was that there was an Ancient who was on the shelf next to me. An Ancient is a very, very old gnome. This one said something to me that I will always

remember. He told me that I was very special indeed because I had been blessed.

"You're lucky, you are," he said. He promised me that we would meet up again in happy times and in a happy place. "You mark my words," he said, and he winked at me.

That's all a very distant memory to me now. I must just tell you about the things that we don't like, then I'll tell you about gnomes and humans and then you'll be able to understand my story properly.

Gnomes hate cats and gnomes hate snakes. We hate them both for the same

good reason. Wherever cats or snakes live there will be very little Naccorom growing. Now, as I told you, Naccorom is the most important thing in the world to gnomes. We have Naccorom if we are feeling a bit fed up and it makes us happy. We have Naccorom when we are happy and it makes us happier still. We make Naccorom tea and, of course, we always fry our fish in Naccorom, so now you know why we hate cats and snakes.

Gnomes hate mini-pixies. Like cats and snakes, mini-pixies stop Naccorom from growing, but worse still they are a working folk. We don't like working and we don't tend to get along too well with folk that do like work, so that is why mini-pixies are our sworn enemies.

We rub along quite nicely with human beings because we don't tend to get in each other's way very much. Human beings do look after gardens and we like that. Most humans think we just stand still all day, but standing still is all most humans see us do so that's why they think that standing still is all we ever do. We actually move and talk and live wonderful lives (unless we get gnomenapped, that is!). The only time that humans can see us or hear us is during the darkest hour of the night. That is why we have to keep still during the darkest hour of the night because we wouldn't want just any human coming along and finding out that we can walk and talk.

We can let a human know that we can walk and talk but we have to be very careful indeed before we choose a human to make contact with. This is because we can only make ourselves known to ten humans in the whole of our life, after that we go to gnome heaven. We will go to gnome heaven sooner than that if our gnome statue breaks! So now you know why being thrown around by Colin and his yam-yam friends fair frightened the living daylights out of me.

*   *   *   *   *   *

I must tell you about the time I became known to my human. His name is Alistair and I must say he is the best human a gnome could wish for. One night I had been out to a particularly good fish fry. I had told lots of stories and I had listened to some really good stories as well. It was getting quite close to the darkest hour of the night so I was very keen to get back to my stone near the pond in my little garden in Harborne, but I've got to tell you that something most unusual caught my eye. A man was standing in the garden throwing little pebbles up at the window. He was calling to be let in. He did look funny. He was wearing a kilt and he had on a posh shirt and a posh black jacket. He had been out drinking spirituous liquors by the looks of things. He was standing still on one foot but stepping forwards and backwards with the other. He couldn't make anyone from inside come to the window so he threw another pebble up and called a bit harder. Still there was no answer, so then he picked up a pebble that was a bit

bigger. This time when he threw it up he broke the window.

'Flippin' heck,' he said, and he stood and stared at the broken window with his mouth wide open. Then, the next thing to happen was that another human appeared at the window and she threw a bucket of water all over him. Well, he started laughing his head off. He laughed and laughed and laughed, in fact he laughed so much that he fell over onto the lawn. He lay face down on the lawn and carried on laughing there. As he was laughing, he looked over to me and I was laughing as well, then he just started talking to me.

I said, 'How did you know I could talk?' and he said, 'I don't know,' and then he carried on laughing.

To this day I don't know how he knew I could talk, but that's how I got to know my human and his name is Alistair. Alistair comes into the garden to talk to me most evenings and I really look forward to our little chats. He comes out and he has a smoke on his pipe. I told him that in the olden days gnomes used to smoke Naccorom in a pipe but now we know that smoking is bad for you so we drink it in tea. I told Alistair that smoking was bad for humans as well. I told him that it was even worse than drinking spirituous liquors. He nodded to me with a very serious face on him but I don't know if that means that he will actually stop smoking. That's the worst thing about smoking: those who start the filthy habit have a dreadful time stopping it. Then very soon they start coughing and spluttering and, in time, folks actually die from it. And even if they know all of this, they still keep doing it because it's such a hard thing to stop.

I taught him the blessing that we say when we take a drink of Naccorom. He really loved it and now says it with me all the time and, when he says it, he laughs out loud and smacks his knees with his hands.

This is the blessing that we say:-

'Naccorom, Naccorom

Thou, the most resplendent of herbs

Thou blessed herb

Thou comforts and enlivens the soul

Without the risks attendant

Upon spirituous liquors

Gentle herb

Let the florid grape

Yield to thee.'

*   *   *   *   *   *

I loved my time in Harborne before I became known to Alistair, but I loved it even more after I had become known to him. Do you know that from the moment I first spoke to Alistair, to this very moment, I have always enjoyed good gnome fishing in that little garden and there has always been plenty of Naccorom.

Now, gnomes love to tell stories as I told you. I won't be modest. I will tell you the truth. I am quite well known as a storyteller and Alistair often asks me to tell him the story of Great Uncle Sylvester.

When I told him that I was writing my story for humans, he made me promise that I would tell you all about Great Uncle Sylvester. I will tell you all about the things that happened to me but first I'll just tell you this little tale about Great Uncle Sylvester.

This story is set many, many years ago in Ireland. Gnomes in those days were very much like gnomes of today. They loved to fish all day and then they loved to meet up in the evening and enjoy a nice fish fry. Of course they loved to sit around their little fires and tell their stories, but, more than anything else, they loved their precious Naccorom, and they were also very much like the gnomes of today because they hated cats and snakes.

Great Uncle Sylvester lived in a little place called Sixmilecross in County Tyrone in Ireland. Each day, he walked a mile from the little farmyard where he lived, through the country lanes and fields, to go fishing for plump and tasty gnomefish. This was the site of the best gnome fishing in the world. The river Glusha. It's one of those strange words like Naccorom - you don't say it the same way that you spell it. To pronounce the river you say Glushy. The river Glusha and Sixmilecross are the best places in the world for gnomes. There is a big place of worship on a hill with a cemetery that overlooks the main street. Sixmilecross has a wide main street with rows of shops and houses. There was a little oratory there where the priest used to visit and say Mass and a little sweet shop called "Aunt Peggy's". I can tell all humans this: if you want to give the gnome in your garden a real treat take them on holiday to Sixmilecross and let them fish in the Glusha. On one eventful morning, when Great Uncle Sylvester walked down to the Glusha, he came upon a sight that would worry the very bravest of gnomes. He saw a poor little gnome being attacked by a snake. The little gnome had his back pressed up against a tree. He was shivering with fright because a long horrible snake had slithered up to him and was lying in front of him, sticking his horrible tongue in and out at him and frightening him half to death.

Great Uncle Sylvester did something then that was to change his life forever. Without a thought for himself or his own safety, he leapt on the snake's body, just

behind his head. He pulled his fishing rod from behind his back and he reached over in front of the snake's head and used his fishing rod to hold the snake's mouth wide open. Then he did the strangest thing, he reached into the pouch that he had by his side and pulled out a big fresh wad of Naccorom and forced it into the snake's mouth. The snake thrashed around and threw his whole body up and down trying to throw Great Uncle Sylvester off him, but Great Uncle Sylvester would not be moved. Then a few moments later something happened that was to change the whole course of history.

The snake went limp and died.

Great Uncle Sylvester had no idea that Naccorom would kill snakes. Nobody knew. He was never able to tell why he put his Naccorom into the snake's mouth because he never knew why he did it. It was just an impulse. The little gnome that had been under threat that day thanked him profusely and Great Uncle Sylvester continued on his way.

Soon word got around that Great Uncle Sylvester had killed a snake and he became

quite famous among the local gnomes. This was such a newsworthy event, though, that Great Uncle Sylvester's fame was not confined to his little village.

Gradually gnomes began arriving from all over the county and then from all over the country. They all wanted to meet the gnome who killed a snake with Naccorom. Great Uncle Sylvester's fish frying parties became legendary. Gnomes gathered around him nightly, sometimes they travelled for many weeks just to meet him. Always they brought with them plenty of big plump gnomefish and, of course, they always made sure that they had a bountiful supply of the very best Naccorom that they could find. And, night after night, gnomes from here, there and everywhere settled down to recite the ancient blessing.

Naccorom, Naccorom

Thou, the most resplendent of herbs

Thou blessed herb

Thou comforts and enlivens the soul

Without the risks attendant

Upon spirituous liquors

Gentle herb

Let the florid grape

Yield to thee.

(They say that reciting this blessing brings good fortune to gnomes everywhere. I don't know if this works when humans say it but, if you could learn this by heart, and say it every day, you might be making good luck for gnomes!)

The reason that he became so famous for this was because snakes were making it very difficult for gnomes to live. They were stopping Naccorom from growing freely. A group of Ancients from all over Ireland got together one day and went to see Great Uncle Sylvester. They had a proposition for him. They asked him to lead them in a crusade against the snakes. They wanted brave gnomes from all over Ireland to come together and wage war against these vile, hard-skinned, legless lizards.

The idea took Great Uncle Sylvester by surprise. Gnomes were not fighting folk, it just wasn't in their nature. Fishing and telling stories were what gnomes did. The trust that gnomes great and good from all over Ireland put in him touched him greatly and, although he had to think about it hard and long, he did eventually agree to lead the gnomes in a bid to free Ireland from snakes.

This was the start of one of the longest and hardest wars in the history of Ireland. In fields and hillsides, from Malin to Crookhaven, brave gnomes lured snakes out to confront them and gnomes who were braver still leapt on them and forced their precious Naccorom into their mouths.

After many ferocious battles of flood and field, of hair-breadth escapes from the deadly foe, of fortunes ill and fair, of sieges long and short from rough quarries, rocks and hills whose heads touched heaven, it came to pass that there were no more snakes left to fight. Great Uncle Sylvester had led the gnomes of Ireland in an effort to rid the Emerald Isle of snakes. He had succeeded. They were happy times. Ireland had become a land free of snakes and Great Uncle Sylvester had become the greatest hero in Irish history.

Alistair told me that humans believe that St Patrick got rid of the snakes in Ireland. What a cheek! It was Great Uncle Sylvester and no mistake. If you ever hear humans saying otherwise, you be sure and tell them the truth! You tell them that Lucky the Gnome knows the real truth and it was not St Patrick at all (noble and glorious saint though he is, I'm sure). No, you tell them that Great Uncle Sylvester got rid of all the snakes in Ireland. Alistair will tell any human that he meets and so you should too!

*   *   *   *   *   *

Great Uncle Sylvester grew old in glorious style. The fame that he had known as the gnome who killed a snake was insignificant compared to the fame that he enjoyed as the gnome who rid Ireland of its snakes, but the days of plenty that Great Uncle Sylvester and his contemporaries enjoyed, sadly, didn't last forever.

Dark days descended on Ireland. At first there was a weak crop of Naccorom and, the following year, the herb that the gnomes loved so much suffered further still. Fish fries became joyless affairs. No gnomes wanted to listen to stories and even if they did, no gnomes wanted to tell them anyway. Eventually the entire crop of Naccorom failed and a gloom fell over the country. It was the saddest of times. Gnomes the length and breadth of Ireland knew that they had to leave the country that they loved so much. They set off with heavy hearts, some to the United States of America, some to Holland and some to countries where no gnome had gone before. Many a tear fell softly on the shores of Ireland as the gnomes whispered fond farewells to those who set off in search of Naccorom. Even Great Uncle Sylvester felt the need to seek a new life abroad.

It was this that led Great Uncle Sylvester to England. There were Naccorom fields of plenty here and, like many others of his generation, Great Uncle Sylvester settled into an altogether happier way of life than the one he had left behind.

48

*   *   *   *   *   *

There's one thing that you can be certain of where gnomes are concerned, and that is that, wherever there are gnomefish and Naccorom, there will always be fish fries and stories. It didn't take long for the word to pass from campfire to campfire that Great Uncle Sylvester had settled in England. In time, the gnome leaders of England came to call upon Great Uncle Sylvester, just like their Irish counterparts had done before them. Harborne was a quiet village in the middle of Birmingham, which is in the middle of England. That is where I live, but Great Uncle Sylvester lived in a place called Solihull, which was not very far from Birmingham at all. It is a place that gnomes love to visit today. They like to be able to say that they have been to the place where great Uncle Sylvester had lived all those years ago. Actually, if you search Solihull very carefully you might find the statue that gnomes have erected in Great Uncle Sylvester's memory. It's in a garden with lots of roses, some red and some yellow, and underneath it was written the sacred blessing:

Naccorom, Naccorom

Thou, the most resplendent of herbs

Thou blessed herb

Thou comforts and enlivens the soul

Without the risks attendant

Upon spirituous liquors

Gentle herb

Let the florid grape

Yield to thee

and then it has these words under that:

In memory of Great Uncle Sylvester

"The bravest gnome who ever lived".

The English gnomes too had a request

to make of him. The challenge that they had

in store for him was even more dangerous

IN MEMORY OF
GREAT UNCLE SYLVESTER...
"The greatest gnome
whoever lived."

and more difficult than ridding Ireland of snakes had been. They wanted Great Uncle Sylvester to lead the English gnomes against the mini-pixies.

Great Uncle Sylvester was already an old gnome and something like this was really a job for younger gnomes. He told them all that he was very touched by the faith that they had put in him, but he declined to help them. The gnome leaders of England were not put off though, they told Great Uncle Sylvester that they feared for their future if the mini-pixies were not engaged in battle.

The problem was this: many new gnomes were arriving in England from Ireland with almost each passing day. There were also gnomes coming into England from Scandinavia and India. At that time, there was enough Naccorom for every gnome, but with so many new gnomes, they feared for the future.

Mini-pixies were the kiss of death for Naccorom. Wherever they lived, Naccorom wouldn't grow for miles and miles. Mini-pixies lived by the legend of the Catchew. Catchews are huge statues of cats and mini-pixies believe them to be sacred. They put

Catchews in their Inner Sanctum. To get to them you need to go deep into huge passageways cut into the rock face and climb high up to the altar-like place where they are kept.

Mini-pixies believe that Catchews look over them and that they needed to live in the shadow of a Catchew or they would perish and die. A great tribe of mini-pixies lived in the middle of England and the gnome leaders knew that ridding that place of mini-pixies would mean that vast new areas of land would be opened up for gnomes to settle and make a fresh start in life. The only gnome that they knew of who could succeed in such a feat was Great Uncle Sylvester and that is why they asked him to reconsider his decision.

Great Uncle Sylvester thought long and hard; they were asking an awful lot of him. Great Uncle Sylvester told them that he needed time to think. He packed a sturdy leather case full of fresh, beautiful-smelling Naccarom and took himself off up into the hills. He knew that he had to give an awful lot of thought to his dilemma. On the one hand, he didn't want to let down all of the gnomes that had put so much faith in him, but, on the other hand, he didn't want to be the gnome who led gnomes into a perilous battle that could cost many of them their lives. Maybe he was just too old for an adventure of such magnitude. Yes, maybe he was just too old: plain and simple.

Great Uncle Sylvester made himself a little camp up in the hillside. He lit a little fire and lay back on a little rock surrounded by long grass. He stayed there in splendid isolation contemplating the most important decision of his life. He resorted to an old habit that he had long since tried to break. He took from his pocket a long, thin clay pipe and filled it full with precious Naccorom. Like many Ancients he had come to realise that smoking was the most dreadful habit a gnome could ever take up. But it is the same for gnomes as it is for humans, once you start the filthy habit, it's devilishly hard to give it up. Sometimes, Great Uncle Sylvester thought to himself that giving up smoking was like learning to clap with one hand. The best thing to do is never to start the filthy habit in the first place. Great Uncle Sylvester blew little bluey grey circles in the air. He put one hand behind his head and lay back against his little rock. He could hear birds singing in the distance and watched the clouds swirling in patterns of white and blue. He felt as though the birds were singing just for him. His mind drifted to his native land. He smiled happily to himself as he thought of all the fish fries. In his mind's eye, he could see laughing gnomes raising cups of Naccorom and singing songs. He could hear the stories as though for the first time. He stood up and took a huge puff from his pipe and shouted out to all of the surrounding hills and valleys:

"Naccorom, Naccorom

Thou, the most resplendent of herbs

Thou blessed herb

Thou comforts and enlivens the soul

Without the risks attendant

Upon spirituous liquors

Gentle herb

Let the florid grape

Yield to thee.

How can I let mini-pixies roam on these pleasant pastures green? I must stand tall, yes, stand tall for good honest gnomes and fear no evil, though we must walk into the shadow of the mini-pixies' Inner Sanctum. The shadows where no Naccorom grows, but where, one day, there will be fields of plenty. Though I am in my dotage, I pledge with the very last breath within me to fight this insolent foe, to face them and force them to flee."

Great Uncle Sylvester felt a little unsteady on his feet, so he sat back down on his rock. He giggled a little to himself because he was happy and slowly fell off to sleep.

When morning came, Great Uncle Sylvester was filled with a renewed vigour. His body, like his spirit, was filled with a youthful vitality. He had made his mind up.

He was to become a great leader of gnomes once again. He cleared away his camp and decided to make haste down towards his home where he planned to gather the most courageous group of gnomes ever to collect together in one place and for one perilous purpose: the crusade against the mini-pixies. Great Uncle Sylvester had only one negative thought in his mind. He felt disgusted with himself for having smoked his pipe and made a promise to himself that he would never succumb to the temptation to smoke again.

When he arrived back home, there were many gnomes who had gathered from far and wide who were waiting to hear his decision. Great Uncle Sylvester made a statement saying that he would lead an expedition against the mini-pixies – on one condition. That condition was that at least fifty gnomes would need to sign up to join him. He posted a notice for gnomes to sign up if they were willing to follow him into battle. The notice said that any gnome wishing to join him would need to sign the notice within seven days.

Great Uncle Sylvester doubted that fifty gnomes would be prepared to follow him. Gnomes were most definitely not fighting folk and mini-pixies would certainly be extremely formidable foes. After waiting for seven days, Great Uncle Sylvester returned to see how many gnomes had added their names to the list. When he arrived there, he couldn't believe the sight that met his eyes. Over five hundred gnomes had signed up to join him. Great Uncle Sylvester shook his head in disbelief. He stroked his long, grey beard and contemplated the future. The future was

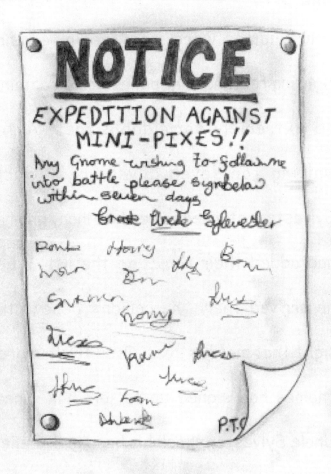

either going to hold very good times for gnomes or it might hold very bad times. Even Great Uncle Sylvester wasn't sure which it would be. He posted another notice - this one told all those gnomes who had resolved to follow him into battle exactly where and when they should assemble.

*   *   *   *   *   *

It was a brisk autumnal morning when Great Uncle Sylvester stood before his new army for the first time. He stood on top of a hill and looked out at the most glorious sight a gnome could see. Before him gathered an enthusiastic band of gallant gnomes. None of them brave or warrior-like in nature, but each and every one of them prepared to follow Great Uncle Sylvester wherever he would lead them. There were hundreds and hundreds of eager gnomes gathered there. Some climbed on the shoulders of others to get a look at Great Uncle Sylvester. Some climbed on fences and more still climbed up on trees and hung precariously off branches.

"My word," he said. "You are a fine body of gnomes. I'm proud of you, each and every one of you. I could not be more proud of you. Gnomes are not warrior folk, we never have been, it's not our way. I, for one, hope that we never will be."

A light murmur went around the vast crowd. They had all heard of his exploits in Ireland, that is why they were there. They knew he was being modest.

"Yes, there have been times when circumstances have forced us into action," he continued. "But only when our very way of life is threatened will we ever raise a hand in anger. It is because we are not fighting folk that I am so proud to stand in front of you today. If we were skilled in the ways of war, it would take little bravery at all to stand where you are standing. If we were not going to face a foe as strong and warlike as the mini-pixies then, yes, that would make it easy to stand where you are standing, but, as we are no more war-like than we are work-like then yes! Yes! I am right to be proud. Every single one of you is showing great, great bravery. By standing where you are today, you are showing bravery worthy of a thousand medals, but it is not medals that we rise for today, no, today we rise for something far more important than mere trifles such as medals. Today, we few, we glorious few, we stand for our very way of life, we stand here not just for ourselves and our way of life but for gnomes everywhere."

All the gnomes there present burst into spontaneous cheers. Some hugged each other and others threw their hats in the air. As a hush descended upon the crowd again, Great Uncle Sylvester returned to his theme.

"I want all of you now present to take from your pouches, your pockets or your purse, one good handful of Naccorom, hold it in front of you, look at it, smell it, hold it firmly in your hands. That, good and true

gnomes, that is why we stand here today. That is why we are prepared to make a stand against the mini-pixies. It is the very stuff of life that we have come to fight for."

Once again a spontaneous cheer went up among the crowd. Some threw their shining bright red caps into the air. Old gnomes did little dances where they stood and younger gnomes rolled up their sleeves and took deep breaths. From within the swelling throng of gnomes. a voice rang out, "Three cheers for Great Uncle Sylvester!

Hip! Hip!" and half a thousand rowdy voices

sang out in response, "Hooray!"

"Hip! Hip!"

"Hooray!"

"Hip! Hip!"

"Hooray!"

Great Uncle Sylvester spoke again, "Let

not this tide of emotion carry you away. Be

of true heart, we are not fighting folk. Let

any gnome here present who has no stomach

for the fight walk freely away from us now.

To do so is to endure no disgrace. To be

carried thus far by heart rather than brain

is indeed a reflection of a strong heart

rather than a weak brain, so leave now, any gnome among you who has a will so to do and your passage from these ranks, I promise you, will be a silent one."

He paused to allow freedom of passage to any gnome who wished to leave. When the stillness became resolute and firm he spoke again.

"Put your hands upon your chest and feel the beating of a hero's heart. Feel the rising and the falling of a hero's chest; feel the power and the glory and be prepared to follow me. Follow me o'er hill and down dale, follow me in country and in town, follow me in fair weather and in foul. Follow me good gnomes, brave and true, follow me into the very pages of history! Future generations shall know your names as well as they know their own. Stories will be told about you whenever fires are lit and fish are fried. Songs will be sung about you. Each year on the anniversary of this day, young gnomes will once more entreat you to tell again the tales of how you walked with old Sylvester into battle. Once more they will ask you to roll back your sleeve or unbutton your shirt so that they may see the scars of battle again and that, though they may be faded, they be worn with dignity and pride, worn in memory of this day of destiny. Now is the hour! Now is our time! Carpe diem!!!"

Roars and cheers rang out around the fields and every gnome there present rallied to the call and with, one small step, Great Uncle Sylvester began the longest march in gnome history.

*   *   *   *   *   *

For many days and many nights they followed him. The journey that he took them on was many miles long. They waited up at night time and made camp. They split up into small groups and lit small fires. If

only humans could see this sight, they would

be spellbound. Small campfires embroidered

the landscape. Gnome camps were set up under trees, alongside hedges and by rivers. It was an impressive sight and no mistake. They fried their gnomefish and drank mugs of hot Naccorom tea. An old Irish gnome played "Danny Boy" on the violin and a friend stood at his side and sang the words as though they were a sacred song. Applause came from around the fields and the passing of the lament signalled a well-earned bed time. The gnomes, one by one, lay down their weary heads and gently fell off to sleep. In the morning, Great Uncle Sylvester gave instructions for gnomes to work in groups

of ten to practise carrying big logs or small trees above their heads. None of them knew why they were being asked to do this but, such was their faith in their leader, that each and every one of them did it to the best of their ability.

Evening camps and morning training passed between miles of hiking and eventually they settled as close to the mini-pixies' Inner Sanctum as they dared.

Great Uncle Sylvester gathered his army around him to tell them of his plans. There was a feeling of great expectancy as the gnomes shuffled forward to listen to him. Some climbed onto branches of nearby trees, some found little rocks to sit on, but many simply stood on the grass and waited. Great Uncle Sylvester told them that it was too dangerous for gnomes to stay around these parts for too long so the time of the raid would be that very night. He told them that he needed two volunteers; he impressed upon them that they would have to make a great personal sacrifice and may even be called upon to make the ultimate sacrifice for their fellow gnomes. He stood and waited a while to let the gravity of his words sink in. He then told them that if there were two gnomes there present willing to make such a sacrifice then they should take one step forward. Just as he had done when he first met them, Great Uncle Sylvester put his hands on his hips and threw his shoulders back. Even he could barely believe his eyes as every gnome in front of him took a step forward. He wore a big smile on his face and he said, "My word, gnomes, you make me proud." He reached out his hands to two young fit gnomes in the front and pulled them up close to him. He told them that they could be the ones to take on this special

mission that night and every gnome clapped and cheered them. Then Great Uncle Sylvester told them of his plan.

"Tonight," he said, "we're going to carry out the most daring raid in history. These two fine examples of gnomes will distract every human, cat, snake and mini-pixie, here about, whilst we will enter the mini-pixies' inner chamber and steal away their Catchew."

A communal gasp went around the gnomes. The idea of gnomes stealing a Catchew right from the inner chamber of the mini-pixies was a thought that made their mouths go dry and their hands go wet.

"When the sky goes dark," Great Uncle Slyvester continued, "and upon my signal, these two fine gnomes will run out into the open and make themselves known to every human that they see. In the chaos that is sure to follow, a courageous regiment of gnomes will follow me into the Inner Sanctum and we will steal their Catchew from under their very eyes. Then we will hide it in a hedge near the farmyard." He pointed over towards a nearby farm. "As soon as it is safe to move, we will hide the

Catchew down the well in the farmyard. Then, as soon as safety permits us, we will take turns to carry the Catchew above our heads in groups of ten. We will carry it all the way back to Birmingham. There is a great lake there which will be a watery grave for that Catchew. We will take a boat and row out into the middle of the lake and drop the Catchew into it. This area has been chosen because it is a barren place for Naccorom and will cause the least distress to gnomes. The mini-pixies will of course leave this place without the Catchew to protect them. Gradually gnomes will come to populate the area and Naccorom will grow freely. Rest up now, put Naccorom and gnomefish a-plenty in your pouches. Be strong, my gnomes, be strong, away now and stay safe until the alarm be raised."

The gnomes drifted away to rest up as Great Uncle Sylvester had advised them. Some lay in ditches, some sat on the hillside and chatted. Tense hours lay ahead of them. Another Irish gnome had made the journey and he perched himself on a low branch of a little willow tree. He played a haunting tune on his flute. It was just about the only sound that rested on the quiet air that evening. Gradually, the sun fell from the sky, the evening air grew cooler and dusk settled on the hillsides. It was time.

Upon Great Uncle Sylvester's signal the two young volunteer gnomes sprang into action. They ran out into the sleeping village squares and sang and danced for all their worth.

"Here we are," they shouted. "Look at us! Come and get us."

"Ha! Ha! Ha!"

"Wake up, you sleepy heads."

"Wake up!"

Humans who heard the commotion came running out to see what it was. Those first lucky ones who saw the gnomes raised an alarm that was fit to waken the dead.

"Gnomes Alive!" they shouted. "Come quick, come quick! Everybody! Come and see. There are gnomes here who are walking and talking!"

Women screamed and jumped on walls. Shopkeepers fetched their brooms. Farmers came running from the public house and shouted, "Fetch your guns! Fetch your guns!" An old man wandered out of the public house with a large glass of foaming spirituous liquor in his hand. He saw one of the gnomes duck down under a cart and run away. He looked at his drink and shook

his head. He put it down on the ground and

walked away from it.

"Never again," he said. "Never again will a drop of spirituous liquor pass my lips". He wandered off down the street. He gave a little hiccup and straightened his hat.

"Keep them alive," a voice shouted. "They're worth a fortune."

Humans were running in all directions. A gaggle of geese nearby were disturbed and they jumped in the air and squealed and squawked. You have never heard such a commotion in your life.

Mini-pixies heard that there were gnomes about and they each wanted to be the one who captured them. Cats wanted to crawl up next to them and rub their vile fur in their faces and breathe their cat breath over them.

The two gnomes fled for their lives. One flew onto a passing cart and hid under some straw. The other jumped over a hedge and hid underneath some flowers.

Great Uncle Sylvester brought two and twenty gnomes with him and entered the rocks where the mini-pixies had their Catchew hidden in their Inner Sanctum, other gnomes hid out in their prepared hiding places waiting for their turn to help in moving the Catchew to safety.

Inside the rocks, they found a long set of steps leading up to an altar. High up inside the cave, they could see lights coming from many candles. They surrounded the great figure of the Catchew. It was perhaps a little smaller than a human but it certainly looked very sleek and impressive. It was a giant sized statue of a sleek and slender cat with black fur. He had white feet and long whiskers.

The cats and the mini-pixies who normally stood guard had all left. They had been unable to contain themselves once they knew there were gnomes about. The steps were too large for the gnomes to run up but they did clamber up them as quickly as they could. They had to carry long ropes with them. Puffing and panting, Great Uncle Sylvester led his followers up to the feet of the Catchew and began climbing up its sides. He wrapped the rope around its neck and abseiled back down again. Together they pulled down and caught it as it fell. The gnomes formed themselves into two columns, they lifted the Catchew above their heads and carried it down the big steps and out to the opening in the rocks. They peered into the open air and, when they were sure

that there were no enemies about, they dragged it down the hillside and across the fields to the ditch that was to be its temporary hiding place.

The plan was to hide out in the ditch until the farmyard was clear of cats and mini-pixies, then, before the darkest hour of the night, they planned to lower the Catchew down into the well and return for it when all of the commotion had died down. All they would have to do was stay hidden from the mini-pixies, well away from cats and to make sure that they were perfectly still during the darkest hour so that no humans saw them.

The darkest hour was fast approaching and the gnomes were huddled in place, hiding in the ditch by the farm. They could see the well where they planned to hide the Catchew, but the farmer and his son stood right on top of it, leaning on the well wall and talking. The farmer had been one of the humans who had seen the gnomes move and he had been frantically running all around the village and the surrounding areas trying to seek them out. He was telling his son over and over again just what they looked like. He was telling him what he would do if he caught one. He said that he would tour the world showing him to people. He said that he would charge people a fortune to see him sing and dance. He was almost crying as he told his son that it would mean an end to all of their problems. He said that they could live like kings for the rest of their lives and never have to work again.

Great Uncle Sylvester was telling his followers that all they needed to do was stay hidden for just a little longer and everything would be all right. A gnome crawled along the ditch and came up close to Great Uncle Sylvester; he was losing his nerve.

"This is madness," he pleaded. "We can't stay here any longer, we could be captured by mini-pixies or sniffed out by cats at any minute. The plan was good, but nobody could have guessed that the farmer and his son would be standing by the well. We should be far away from here and in our hiding places now. The darkest hour will be upon us soon, we must leave now, leave the Catchew here, we'll all be doomed if we stay."

Great Uncle Sylvester put his arm on the gnome's shoulder and told him to steady his nerve.

"We've got time," he said. "We've got another ten minutes before the darkest hour, if we can avoid cats and mini-pixies for the next two or three minutes, we can still move the Catchew to the well. All we need is for the farmer and his son to move away from the well. Just hold your nerve for a little longer."

The moon was dull as the darkest hour approached. The well was in the middle of a gravel-filled yard. There was little or no

protection from sight. The gnomes all knew that the chances of hiding the Catchew successfully and getting away were fading fast.

Two minutes passed, then three, then four. The farmer and his son walked over to the fence at the far side of the farmyard. If only they were to have gone inside, the mission could have continued, but they didn't, they leant up against the fence and lit up their pipes. The farmer's wife brought out two foaming pints of spirituous liquors.

Great Uncle Sylvester looked all around. Every gnome that he could see was watching him closely, waiting to find out what was going to happen next. He sent a message down the line.

"The mission is going ahead."

One by one the gnomes passed on the message in a solemn whisper.

"The mission is going ahead."

"The mission is going ahead."

Great Uncle Sylvester turned to two gnomes who were crouched down in the trench near him. He told them that the darkest hour was upon them, but he asked if they were prepared to take on a very dangerous job. They nodded back eagerly and Great Uncle Sylvester told them what to do. They were to sneak around to the far side of the farmyard and frighten all of the chickens into making a whole lot of noise.

Without a moment's thought to their own safety, they started off to crawl around to the chicken coop.

"Be very careful now, gnomes, we are in the darkest hour and, if you are spotted by one of the humans, you will be putting us all in danger of our lives." They promised him that they would be careful and they set off on their task.

Great Uncle Sylvester sent a fresh message down the line. The rest of them were going to carry the Catchew over the farmyard and lower it down the well as soon as the chickens caused an uproar and drew the farmer and his son away from the farmyard.

The gnomes couldn't believe what they were hearing. It was madness. No gnomes ever moved during the darkest hour – ever! If the humans didn't see them the mini-pixies were bound to and it wouldn't be very long

before they found out that the Catchew had been stolen and then all hell would be let loose.

A sudden loud squawking by the chickens shattered the stillness of the night. The farmer and his son went to investigate. The son suggested that it might be the gnomes again but the farmer said that they would be long gone by now. He said that it was much more likely to be the work of foxes.

Great Uncle Sylvester and his band of followers sprang into action. They lifted the Catchew up above their heads and rushed with it over the ground and began the job of hauling it up over the well wall. Some gnomes pushed from underneath and others got up onto the well wall and dragged it upwards. One of the gnomes was so eager that he toppled over the side and, but for a very quick acting friend, he would have fallen down the long dark shaft and been lost in cold murky waters below. One gnome caught a hold of his coat and two others pulled him back to safety. They leaned the statue over the top of the wall and started lowering it down.

The chickens had calmed down by now and the farmer and his son started to return to their spirituous liquors.

Great Uncle Sylvester was lowering the Catchew down into the water when some of the gnomes started telling him to let it drop; they told him that the humans were returning. Great Uncle Sylvester kept on lowering the rope, he told them that if they were to let it drop, the splash would attract the attention of the humans and they would all be caught.

The farmer and his son returned to leaning on the fence and drinking their spirituous liquors.

The Catchew was slowly slipped into the water and Great Uncle Sylvester and the gnomes, still standing on the top of the well wall, allowed themselves a little smile. They couldn't afford to walk back over the gravel of the courtyard because it would make too much noise. Instead they signalled back to the gnomes in the ditch. Their plan was to throw the rope over to the other gnomes. They knew that one of the gnomes might have to sneak half way across the yard with it. The other gnomes would have to crawl along the rope if they were to get free. It was a long way for a gnome to crawl along on a rope, but there was no other way.

One by one, they made their way back across the courtyard by pulling themselves along the rope. One slip would mean that they would all certainly be found. They couldn't risk staying where they were, though. The mini-pixies would find out that their Catchew had been stolen any time now and they were sure to search in every nook and cranny that they could find to try and retrieve it. Eventually every last gnome reached the far end of the farmyard.

Great Uncle Sylvester undid the rope and beckoned his comrades to pull it home. He crouched down perching on uneven bricks on the inside of the well wall. He waited with all the stillness that he could muster. He knew that any slip or sound would attract the farmer and his son and he would be drowned. Never before had Great Uncle Sylvester or any of his comrades looked forward to the ending of the darkest hour with such grave anticipation. As great Uncle Sylvester settled himself down, the other gnomes knew exactly what it was they had to do. They waited and hid in silence.

Great Uncle Sylvester and his followers showed all of the discipline and patience that they needed. By the end of the darkest hour, the farmer and his son had returned into their house. Now the gnomes had to hide out for two days, after that they would all meet up again to retrieve the Catchew and take it to its watery grave. This would give time for the mini-pixies to stop their search and to be thinking of heading off to look for it elsewhere.

The following days were filled with mixed emotions for the gnomes. They were proud of their achievements so far, but they knew that every mini-pixie in the area was out looking for them and they knew also that they still had the task of getting the Catchew all the way back to Birmingham.

Every single hiding place that you could possibly think of was taken up by the gnomes; even the gnomes who managed to get quite far away still kept in hiding places. Very few stories were told and even fewer fires were lit. For most, it was the loneliest and most miserable two days of their life, but they knew that their cause was noble and so they endured their hardship willingly.

When the appointed hour came, they met up again; seeing all the other gnomes somehow gave them courage. The mini-pixies had been furious at the loss of their Catchew and they presumed that it was some human that had found out about their Inner Sanctum and had stolen it. They never dreamt that gnomes would ever have the courage to do such a thing.

The long march back to Birmingham was easier than any of them had ever imagined. They took it in turns to work in teams of ten, holding the Catchew up above their heads, and in relays of a mile at a time. They marched all the way back with a considerable spring in their steps. When they reached Birmingham, they took the Catchew in a rowing boat and rowed out to the middle of a great lake and dropped it to the bottom where it rests until this day. Humans have built a set of motorways near that lake and they've called it Spaghetti Junction. If you are ever near there look out for the lake because that is where the mini-pixies' Catchew lies to this very day.

The mini-pixies soon split up. They fell out amongst themselves and many of them blamed each other for the loss of the Catchew. All of them left. They believed in the folklore that said mini-pixies could not live unless they were in the presence of a Catchew to look over them.

Great Uncle Sylvester and his brave followers had been magnificent. They had achieved real greatness. They had opened up new areas to grow Naccorom and gnomes from all over the world had a new place to settle in. Great Uncle Sylvester had promised them the status of heroes and he was right. Their names became household names and invitations to their fish fries became the most sought after commodity after Naccorom itself.

Now I know that they were very brave gnomes indeed and what they achieved was marvellous. Nothing short of marvellous! But at least they knew what they were letting themselves in for. When I was gnomenapped I had no idea of what was in store for me. I promised you that I would tell you about my ordeal and now I will.

*   *   *   *   *   *

I was trembling with fear on the morning

that they gnomenapped me and put me on the floor of their car. Normally I would think of laughter as being a nice sound but the sound of them laughing in that car was the worst sound that I had ever heard.

They took me to lots of famous places. They took me to the Tower of London and to Buckingham Palace and they took my photograph in front of them. They used to put a newspaper next to me to show what the date was and then they would send the picture to Alistair with a ransom note. They said that if Alistair would send them one million pounds then they would return me

to him. This was a really cruel thing to do because they knew he could never pay them a million pounds. Everywhere that they took me they used to put me on the table with all of their glasses full of spirituous liquors. They used to get drunk and talk very loudly and pass me around from human to human. It was a horrible time. It really was.

Then things got even worse. They took me off to France and they did the same things there. It was the first time that I had been on a boat. This was horrible as well. Being indoors is vile for gnomes. Then when we got to France, they took me to

the Arc de Triomphe and to the Eiffel Tower and they took my photograph in front of them. They sent the pictures back to Alistair and sent him more ransom notes. I felt really sorry for myself but I felt really sorry for Alistair as well. He must have been very upset. Every night when I was lonely and indoors and away from home I used to think about Alistair wandering out into his garden and me not being there. I used to think of him sitting down by the pond and not having me to talk with. It made me really sad.

I didn't know that I could get any sadder than I was at that time but I could. Colin and his yam-yam friends took me off to the United States of America. They followed the same pattern that they had done in England and France. They took their photographs in front of the Empire State Building and other famous places. Then they took me out with them and put me on their table when they had their spirituous liquors. In one of the bars in New York, they put me under their table and when they went home at the end of the day they left me there.

Once I realised that they had left me alone in a foreign place I became as sad, I think, as a gnome could ever be. There was a waiter there who took me home with him. I knew then that I would probably never see my little garden in Harborne again. Oh, how my heart yearned for that little garden in Tansoo House again! More importantly, I knew that I would probably never see Alistair again. The waiter took me home and kept me. He didn't have a garden. He put me in a little window box with a couple of flowers.

Well, you can imagine how I felt. I had no way of making my way back to Harborne. I was stuck in the little window box. All I could see from where I was living was buildings and cars and people. I could hardly see any green at all. If I wanted to go fishing and find some Naccorom I had an awful job. I had to climb down some metal steps and I had to walk down the busy streets and dodge in and out of people's legs. Then I had to get across busy roads full of cars and taxi cabs. Let me tell you the plain awful truth. Whenever a gnome finds somewhere to fish in New York, he

can expect to stay there for hours and hours or even days and never catch a fish. There's precious little Naccorom in New York. I saw some gnomes standing on a roof smoking it once. I couldn't believe my eyes. I just looked the other way. I pretended that I hadn't seen them and I just carried on my way home. New York may be a really nice place for humans to live but it is a really bad place for gnomes. Fancy gnomes smoking in this day and age when they know all the harm it could do to your health. Oh! The very thought of it makes me want to be sick.

For the most part of my life in New York, I just used to sit in my little window box looking out at the busy streets and feeling homesick for my little garden in Harborne and for my human, Alistair.

A bright part of my life came when a new family moved into the area. They were from Scandinavia and they were very nice indeed. I used to go and have fish fries with them very often and they made me most welcome. There was a gnome and his gnome wife and their son. They had discovered a well near a shopping mall and very early in the morning they used to go over there and

catch some fish. It didn't take them very long at all to catch some fish there. I was very impressed. The fish were not huge, but they were good gnomes and they were always happy to share what little gnomefish they had. For a while they made me nice cups of Naccorom tea and I was ever so grateful, but I asked them where they found it. I said that I would gladly go on an expedition each day and go and find some so that I could use it for our fish fries. They were a little bit ashamed to tell me at first, but they used to get their Naccorom by bartering. They had to go out and give some local fish in exchange for Naccorom. I was a little bit taken aback, I can tell you. These were not gnome ways at all. It was indeed a strange time and a strange place to be a gnome. What Naccorom we could get was not very good quality at all, to be honest. Although it was, of course, a lot better than not having any Naccorom at all, it was not really the same.

We did have some good fish fries just the same. I took my turn in bartering. It was quite an unpleasant thing to do; I used to have to climb over the roofs of several homes and then make my way down an old fire escape on the side of a building. I had to walk along an old alleyway with lots of bins and cardboard and stuff on the ground. We would call it rubbish but they called it garbage. They have different words for lots of things. They called the pavement a sidewalk, for instance. When I walked down the alleyway, I would have to knock on an old piece of corrugated iron. A young gnome would poke his head out of the side of it but he wouldn't say anything. He would just look all around to make sure that I was alone. Then a few moments later, a big gnome would step out. He wore dark glasses and a gold ring and a gold tooth. I didn't like him at all. But if you wanted some Naccorom in those days, this was just about the only way that you could get it. I used to try and get as much Naccorom as I could for as little gnomefish as I could. I didn't feel very comfortable doing it, but that was just the way things were.

I did have some very pleasant fish fries with that nice Scandinavian family. There were some nice Armenian gnomes who lived in the area and we sat for many long hours telling our stories. Of course, they loved me to tell them stories about Great Uncle

Sylvester and, of course, I used to love to tell them.

The Scandinavians don't have a hero like Great Uncle Sylvester to talk about but they do have lots of stories about wood carvers. Their Ancients used to carve beautiful designs out of wood. They made little fish. They made real working swings. They made little wooden clogs that gnomes could actually use. They made furniture and they made beautiful fairy tale towers. When the nice Scandinavian family described all these things, I used to take a big drink of Naccorom and lie back with my hands behind my head and dream I was actually living in a wood in Scandinavia. Ah! It makes my eyes moist just to think about it.

The American gnomes had a hero all of their own that they used to tell stories about. I must admit that they were really fantastic stories even though they were very far-fetched. I didn't believe a word of them. They were all about a gnome called Super Gnome. He wore a blue cloak and he used to fly around the skies of New York. If there was ever a gnome in trouble, the Super Gnome used to fly down and save

142

them. He used to fly into the side of cats with such force that he knocked them out. He used to pick snakes up and fling them about his head. Oh, dear me, yes, he could do anything! Do you know that in some stories he used to pick mini-pixies up and fly off with them? They were great stories; I've got to hand it to the Americans, their stories about Super Gnome were really good. Mind you, you wouldn't want to go believing them, though. Some of the Americans did but I didn't. I did used to daydream about how good it would be if it was true. If Super Gnome really did exist, he could swoop down and pick me up and fly me back to my little garden in Harborne. I used to imagine that he would come down and pick me up and fly me over the rooftops and high up into the sky and through the clouds, over the sea back to Birmingham and back to Alistair. Well – it does no harm to dream, does it? Sometimes in times of hardship, it's only our dreams that keep us going, isn't it? But for me to wish that Super Gnome was real and that he would fly down and protect me was a bit like a human wishing that they could find a walking, talking gnome. I know that lots of humans

dream and dream but very few are fortunate enough to find one.

You might think that things couldn't have got much worse for me but they did. The man who put me in his window box gave me to another human and he took me to his home with him. He had a beautiful garden with a long lawn. It had lovely pretty flowers all down the side of it. There was a really nice pond at the back of it and a swing and a garden shed. When I saw it I could barely believe my eyes. It was beautiful. It was really, really beautiful, but that's what made the thing that happened next even worse.

He took me down his garden path and put me in his shed. I couldn't believe it. There I was right next to the most beautiful garden that I had seen in many a long day and I was locked in a shed! I could actually see out of the window all the beautiful flowers and the birds. I could only imagine what beautiful, beautiful, gorgeous, gorgeous, big, plump, fresh gnomefish were swimming about in the pond and I could actually see long, thick, green Naccorom winding its way up the fence. Oh! Let me tell you, it was beautiful and awful both at the same time. And to make things even worse, a cat decided to come to the shed from time to time. It was a vile ginger cat with a white chest. He used to come in the night when it was raining. All that wetness all over him made his disgusting cat smell even stronger than usual. He used to step onto a lawn mower and reach his paws up onto the windowsill next to me. He used to touch my face with his whiskers and sometimes he would press his body up against me. One time he even lay down all across me right under my nose and he stayed there for hours and hours on end. Ugghhh!!!! It was disgusting.

After what seemed like an age there, the human came into the shed one day and picked me up. My heart leapt with joy. He brought me out into the garden and the smell of the fresh air was exhilarating! But then he walked up the garden path with me and brought me into the house. It was disastrous. I was thinking, "Please, please, please carry me back outside," but he brought me into his living room. He was talking on the phone. He was looking at me all over and eyeing me up and down and describing every detail about me. Then he started walking back towards the garden with me but he took me into a little outhouse by his kitchen and instead of taking me back outside, he put me in a basket on the front of an old bicycle. Then he just left me there and walked off! I was in the same position again. I could see the beautiful garden and all that tempting Naccorom but I was still stuck indoors.

I couldn't believe my misfortune. I found myself wishing that I had never known Naccorom. I thought that if I had never seen it, I wouldn't be going through this torment now of knowing what I was missing and being able to see it, and yet

being able to do nothing about it. But from that tantalising position, my story was set to take its most dramatic twist.

*   *   *   *   *   *

I was picked up and taken out of that little basket and the things that happened to me were about as shocking as being gnomenapped from my little garden back in Harborne. I was taken inside and I was covered in brown paper and glue and stamps were put all over it. The next thing I knew, I was brought outside and put in a car. I was just thrown on the back seat. I couldn't see anything and I could only hear the car

engine and the sounds of traffic. I was moved from one place to another and all I could think about was feeling just like this when I was gnomenapped. All kinds of things were going through my mind. I had a feeling that I had been put into an aeroplane. Then I was moved from building to building. I think that I spent about two hours on a train. I wondered what was in store for me next. I thought it might be a place even worse than the places I had known in New York. I thought that it might be a place with no other gnomes to tell stories with.

There might be no gnomefish there or worse, no Naccorom for ever!

Eventually I reached a place where a kind man took all of my brown paper off me. Do you know it seemed just as though they were expecting me. I mean – expecting **me** – not just any old gnome. I must tell you now that all my fears were unwarranted. I had been sent to Ireland. Yes, it was the ancestral home of Great Uncle Sylvester himself. And I was quickly placed outside in the most idyllic garden I could possibly imagine.

This life was the most bountiful that I had ever imagined life could be. It was in complete contrast to my austere existence in New York. The garden was attached to a big farm. It had a plush green lawn for as far as you could see. The pond in the garden was more like a small lake. And there were Naccorom fields of gold. Tall thick strong golden stems of Naccorom grew a-plenty in the surrounding fields. They made the green stems of Naccorom, that I had previously known, seem like insignificant weeds. Those golden stems of Naccorom were majestic and strong. Naccorom was so plentiful hereabouts that gnomes could get lost walking in the fields. On a hot sunny afternoon you could cut some large stems of Naccorom down just to make yourself a bed. The fish were so big that if you stayed fishing for a day you would need two sacks to carry them all home.

Irish gnomes are the most hospitable that I have ever met. They could not have made me more welcome. They welcomed me into their garden with open arms. They welcomed me to their fish fries and they made me their guest of honour. They asked me for all sorts of stories. And I can tell

you that, with such an attentive audience, I loved to talk. Irish gnomes can really drink some Naccorom tea as well, I can tell you. My word, they are a breed apart! Everything seems so relaxed. They would happily keep their fish fries going right through the night, even through the darkest hour. I could not get used to it. I kept asking what would happen if a human came along, but they just shrugged their shoulders. They had the kind of attitude that if they got caught alive by a human then they got caught alive. Of course, they kept an eye out and if they heard a sound that might be a human then they just stopped talking and stood still. My, what a wonderful place it was. Sometimes I felt so fortunate that it felt as though I had died and gone to gnome heaven. I remember thinking that it was as though I had swapped my life for a gnome more fortunate than myself. I could not have been happier. The local gnomes told great stories. They talked of the good old days when heroes the likes of Great Uncle Sylvester roamed the land, but they also told sad stories. They told stories about the great Naccorom crop failure and how so many gnome families were torn apart by the disaster. They also sang songs about those dark days. That's really what sets Irish gnomes apart. They love their music and, my word, when they play they make the angels in gnome heaven dance a ballet.

Oh, how I wish that every gnome that ever lived could spend some time in that garden. Many times I thought of the Scandinavian family that had been so kind to me and shared their tiny little gnomefish and their meagre supplies of Naccorom with me. Why on earth I was so fortunate as to be sent here and they were not, I don't know. I can't make sense of life sometimes.

Sometimes there is no sense to be made of it.

What I am going to tell you now will probably seem very, very strange to you. It might sound as though I am a very ungrateful gnome indeed, but do you know I still missed my little garden in Harborne. I still missed Alistair. Of course, a pond full of plump gnomefish and fields of Naccorom of gold are nice. Well, they are more than nice, they are wonderful, but no matter how wonderful a place is, there's no place like home. And when a gnome makes friends with a human in the way that I have with Alistair, well, there's nothing that can match that in this world. Nothing!

One day a human came out into the garden and picked me up. He carried me into the house and put me on the kitchen table. I need not tell you that all sorts of things went through my mind. "I could be kept inside," I thought. Then I thought that I might be sent to some far off land bereft of all those elements that I had become used to having in such abundance. Fear is like fire, you know. If you let it catch light, it can inflame your whole being and trap you in a fiery hell. But I had no need to be frightened.

*   *   *   *   *   *

I thought that my mind was playing a cruel trick on me, but it wasn't. The human voice that I could hear was none other than Alistair's! It was Alistair who had come from England to get me. It was all that I could do not to jump up then and there and talk to him. He picked me up and he held me in his hands and he was saying, "I've found you, I've found you. Everything's going to be all right now!" He took me out into the garden so that we could talk properly.

I have never been as happy in all my life as I was at that precise moment. He told me that he would be taking me home shortly and that nothing bad would ever happen to me again. He said that he would make sure that no gnomenappers would ever lay one finger on me.

I told him all about France and New York. I told him how I had to barter for Naccorom. He told me how worried he had been. It was an emotional time. Do you know - and this is a mark of how nice Alistair is - he told me that if I was going to be happier in Ireland, he wouldn't mind if I wanted to

167

stay there. I told you that he was really nice, didn't I? There aren't many humans who would do that for a walking, talking gnome.

Alistair said that he wanted to call me 'Lucky' on account of just how lucky I had been. I thought that Lucky suited me very well indeed and I have been known as Lucky from that day to this. The waiter who had found me in New York had told his friend all about me. His friend asked for me because his cousin had had a gnome, just like me, gnomenapped. Lo and behold his cousin was none other than Alistair. I believe this was the happiest coincidence in the whole world. You couldn't make a story like that up, could you?

Alistair had arranged for me to be sent to Ireland because a grand gnome convention was being held there. He asked me if I minded if he took me there. Let me tell you, I had lived through so many sad adventures, a happy one would be a delight.

The gnome convention was wonderful. There was a great big field and humans had come together to show each other their gnomes. And there were gnomes a-plenty there. There were big gnomes and small gnomes. There were gnomes ancient and new. There were gnomes from India, Scandinavia and England. Of course there were gnomes from all over Ireland. It was a true festival of gnomes. Alistair bought me a new (very flexible) fishing rod and he bought me a most beautiful little gnomefish pouch that had been made in India. Then he did something that made me the centre of attention. He stood on the stage and held the microphone. Everybody in the field stopped what they were doing and looked at me. I was a little bit embarrassed, if I

am to tell you the truth, but in a nice kind of way though.

I would say that every single human who was there came and had a really close look at me. Some of them started touching me in the hope that I would bring them good luck. They said things like "fancy being taken all that way and meeting up with Alistair's cousin". To tell you the truth, I often have a little chuckle about it myself when I think about it. My word, I was lucky and no mistake!

I was given a place of honour. I was put on a grand table on the back of a big

truck. It had a velvet cloth all over it. Very old Ancients were there and very posh looking they were too. Well, the one that I was stood next to was perhaps the oldest and the poshest of the lot. I felt very honoured to be in such company, I can tell you. And then, just when there was a quiet moment, he lowered his head and he looked over the top of his spectacles and he spoke to me. He said, "Do you remember me?" I didn't, to be honest, but I sort of looked at him quizzically to see if something would jostle my memory.

He just smiled and said, "Well, you were very young when we last met, but I told you that we would meet again in happier times. And I was right! Here we are!" and he gave a little laugh. "I told you that you were blessed," he said. "And I told you that you were lucky. I never knew then just how lucky you would be."

He gave another of his little joyful chuckles and he said, "You be sure that you carry on being lucky." He laughed again. "Try to make it more good luck than bad, though." He laughed and so did I.

I am back in the garden of my little home in Harborne now. Alistair has made the garden really secure now so no humans can get down there; so now we are very safe.

Every night, Alistair and I sit in the garden together and say the sacred words.

"Naccorom, Naccorom

Thou, the most resplendent of herbs

Thou blessed herb

Thou comforts and enlivens the soul

Without the risks attendant

Upon Spirituous Liquors

Gentle Herb

Let the florid grape

Yield to thee."

We say these special words together and we laugh as we drink a nice cup of Naccorom tea.

Now listen to me. Don't go poking and prodding gnomes too much, will you? But do keep an eye out just in case one wants to make contact with you. If you know a human who has a gnome indoors do encourage them to put them outside, won't you? And always try and keep pesky cats away from us. Oh, and don't forget to look out into your garden if ever you're awake during the darkest hour. You never know what you might see. And just in case you don't know, the darkest hour is always the one that comes just before the dawn.

Be lucky !

Also by the same author...

Harriet
the
Horrible

E.R.Reilly

Harriet is a lovely little girl- that is until she
gets upset. Then she dreams up wonderfully
wicked plans to get her own back...Watch out!
That's when nice little Harriet becomes
... Harriet the Horrible!

Harriet
the
Horrible

in
Best Friends

E.R.Reilly

Harriet and Salty have always got up to
lots of mischief but now they are joined
by a new girl in school.
Colleen is Harriet's new best friend and
toether they have a very special mission
in life...

Contact us to order any of these titles.

SANTIAGO PRESS
PO BOX 8808
BIRMINGHAM
B30 2LR

santiago@reilly19.freeserve.co.uk